# What is
# Social Distancing?

## A Children's Guide

by
Lindsey Coker Luckey

Illustrated by
Nav

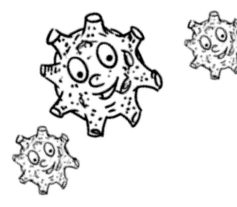

"Logan, I keep hearing about a virus and something called a "pandemic," but I'm not sure what that means. Why can't we go to school? Why can't I see my friends?"

"Carleigh, Sometimes there can be a sickness that goes around that can spread all over the world. That is what is called a pandemic. It is kind of like the flu. It makes you very sick and can be spread easily from person to person."
Luckily, this does not happen very often.

"Is that why I can't go to school?"

"Yes!
Going to school puts you really close to a lot of people. If one person gets the virus, they can easily spread it to so many other kids at school. So it is very important to stay at home to keep us safe!"

"This sounds pretty scary. And I miss my
friends. How long will it be before I can see them again?"

"It can be scary, but that is why it is so important to keep us safe! As long as we take steps to keep us safe, there is no need to be scared. The sooner that we can get everyone well, the sooner we can go back to school and see our friends again!"

"What steps do we need to take to keep us safe?"

"Well, you are already doing the first step by staying at home and away from people! This is what is called "social distancing." We have to "distance" ourselves from other people for a little bit.
It may be hard to be away from friends, but this is what needs to happen so that more people do not get sick! It is also very important that you wash your hands. This is one of the best things that we can do to stay safe."

"Something else: Don't touch your face! Germs can enter through your mouth, nose, and eyes. If you touch something dirty that has germs on it, they can stay on your hands and then if you touch your face, you get sick! This is also why we have to keep our hands washed."

"I don't want germs
on my hands!"

"If we get sick, should we go to the doctor?"

"Not always. Since it is a virus, there is not a lot that a doctor can do to make it go away. It just takes time and a lot of rest. If we get sick, our parents can call the doctor's office and tell them what symptoms we have. They can tell us if we need to go to the doctor or not."

"How do the doctors and nurses not get sick?"

"They do! This is why it is important for us to stay home and only go to the doctor or hospital if it is an emergency. We don't want them to get sick too!"

"Is there anything that we can do to help?"

"Just be grateful for all of the people that are taking care of others. They have to work and not be at home with their families. Maybe we can make them cards or just well-wishes that they stay safe. The best thing that we can do to help is just to stay well ourselves!"

# Activities

# Word Search

```
W u W N Y R K X E K V Q P P I O V O M G
F A Z H R G Z K Y E O W O Z H E C G P X
W D S K T U G S A Z V R R F M V D T Y O
B O P H M B Z R E F K P J B R V O N W U
Q I R G H F Z S W J J T C A J A C K F G
M R P I N A R V E K P Q P S R K T W S Y
O L R Z N U N Z N J H O U C U I O F F H
O D R L N Q I D C T P H G Z S W R G U B
A G Q A J T T A S S V L K F O S X H P N
G T C L I W P Z P B W Y L S U N K Y S A
C W N N I H D L T I U Z P R X Z V R T Z
H V A T J S J W J D P B I Y P O W C A S
Y S Y Z B H Y Q G K P V U N E P C L Y J
D Y M H P C L T Q M P Z R V N A J E S U
A X E W W O S H W A F I F X V N W A A B
L P P Q U P S I I Z N P N J J D E N F I
P F D N X K Y S S X E K M I W E U V E C
T X K X H C P G H E A L T H Y M V R M Z
X T P W O F L I V W P G G G M I P Y B N
J L K Q I F F F Q N N J P Q G C E A P L
```

| | | |
|---|---|---|
| VIRUS | SANITIZE | NURSE |
| WASHHANDS | STAYSAFE | DOCTOR |
| CLEAN | HEALTHY | PANDEMIC |

On which island did the pirates bury their treasure chest? To find out, start from the star in the middle and follow your way around the map using the clues below.

( 1 )  Go left:  $\boxed{4}$ $+ 4 = 8$

( 2 )  Go down: $9 - 5 = \boxed{\phantom{0}}$

( 3 )  Go left: $13 - 7 = \boxed{\phantom{0}}$

( 4 )  Go up: $8 + \boxed{\phantom{0}} = 11$

( 5 )  Go right: $12 - \boxed{\phantom{0}} = 8$

( 6 )  Go up: $6 + \boxed{\phantom{0}} = 9$

( 7 )  Go left: $\boxed{\phantom{0}} + 2 = 9$

( 8 )  Go down: $\boxed{\phantom{0}} + 6 = 13$

( 9 )  Go right: $6 - \boxed{\phantom{0}} = 4$

(10)  Go up: $\boxed{\phantom{0}} + 5 = 11$

(11)  Go right: $11 - \boxed{\phantom{0}} = 5$

(12)  Go down: $15 - \boxed{\phantom{0}} = 8$

(13)  Go right: $11 - \boxed{\phantom{0}} = 7$

(14)  Go up: $15 - 5 = \boxed{\phantom{0}}$

(15)  Go right: $\boxed{\phantom{0}} + 3 = 13$

(16)  Go down: $7 + \boxed{\phantom{0}} = 14$

(17)  Go left: $5 + \boxed{\phantom{0}} = 8$

(18)  Go up: $19 - \boxed{\phantom{0}} = 10$

(19)  Go right: $9 - 3 = \boxed{\phantom{0}}$

(20)  Go down: $\boxed{\phantom{0}} + 5 = 8$

☞ Find your way through the maze, from start to finish.

Start

Finish

# TIC TAC TOE

# Spot the Difference

## FIND THE 5 DIFFERENCES BETWEEN THE ILLUSTRATIONS BELOW

# Spot the Difference

FIND THE 5 DIFFERENCES BETWEEN THE ILLUSTRATIONS BELOW

# Spot the Difference

# COLOR

# COLOR

Made in the USA
Coppell, TX
18 August 2020

33804104R00019